Celebrations

CELESTA THIESSEN
KEZIAH THIESSEN

CONTENTS

HALLOWEEN

"Halloween's coming up soon," said Princess Keziah. She was eight years old and one of the triplets of Kitty Castle. Kitty Castle was a very old castle at the heart of Kitty Kingdom.

Keziah, her two sisters, her two brothers, and her parents were eating supper around a large wooden table in their beautiful dining room. It was nice being all together again. Their parents had just recently returned from a long quest to find a way to defeat the dragons.

"I've been meaning to talk to you about Halloween," said her mother. The queen looked at her children sadly. "There's only enough candy left for each of you to have one piece."

"The dragons burned up all the sugar beet crops so there is no sugar in the entire kingdom. Candy can't be made without sugar. Halloween will have to be cancelled this year," said her father, the king.

"Oh, no!" said Princess Celesta. "Not cancelled! Halloween's my favorite holiday!"

"There's nothing else we can do," said her mother. "You can't have Halloween without candy."

"We could give out cat treats," suggested David. Everyone around the table laughed. "What's so funny? All the cats would love to go trick-or-treating with their owners." David was the youngest of the children. He was only five years old.

The princesses giggled again.

"But I wanted to go trick-or-treating, riding on Charcoal," said Keziah, "and I already decided what I'm going to be. A princess!" Everyone laughed.

"I made my costume already," said Priscilla. "I'm going to be a cat. We can't just cancel Halloween!"

Richard leaned over and whispered to his brother and sisters, "Don't worry. We'll think of something." Richard was their older brother. He was eleven.

At the end of the meal, the queen opened a box that had been sitting on the table in front of her. It contained five different treats. She gave one to each of the children. "This is all the candy that's left in the whole kingdom. Try to enjoy it, Children. You deserve to have it after the good work you did, saving the kingdom from the dragons."

"I get a mini candy cane?" asked David. "Seriously? That's not a Halloween treat!"

"I'll eat it if you don't want it," said Richard.

"Oh, that's ok. I'm not complaining. I like candy canes!" David grabbed his candy as Richard reached for it.

Later that evening, the children went out to look at their garden in the courtyard. Nightcat joined them, after eating his supper in the kitchen with the other cats. Nightcat was a good, magical creature. He looked like a giant silver cat with huge wings and he was as big as a tiger!

"Isn't it weird how, even though it's late fall, almost winter, the plants in our garden are still green and are still producing fruit and vegetables?" said Celesta.

"It must be the magic water that's under Kitty Castle," said Keziah.

"I wonder if *anything* would grow in this garden since it's…well…magical!" said David.

"What are you saying?" asked Keziah.

"I said, 'I wonder if *anything* would grow in this garden?" said David.

"I mean, what do you mean!" said Keziah.

"Oh, I was just wondering…what if I plant my candy cane in the garden? Do you think a candy cane tree would grow? Because, then, we could still have Halloween."

"I think it would!" said Keziah. "I'm going to plant my candy too!"

"That won't work!" said Richard. "Don't waste your candy by burying it in the dirt! There's no such thing as a candy tree!"

"Nightcat, will candy plants grow if we plant our candies?" asked Priscilla.

"I'm not a garden expert," said Nightcat. "I don't know."

"I want everyone to have candy, not just me," said David.

Keziah nodded.

"But what if it doesn't work?" said Priscilla. "Then no one will get candy…and I really like candy."

"Maybe it's worth the risk," said Celesta. "It would be sorta selfish for us to eat candy when no one else can have any."

"And, if it does work, we can have lots of treats instead of just one!" said David. The other children laughed.

Keziah dug in the dirt with her hand and dropped her pink bubble gum into the hole. Then she buried it. "There. Now, by morning, we'll have a pink bubble gum tree that makes bubble fruits!"

"Are you sure about this?" asked Priscilla.

"We have to try," said Keziah.

"I agree," said Celesta. "I'm going to plant my candy too."

David kicked a hole in the dirt with his shoe. Then he dropped his candy cane in and kicked a small mound of mud over top of it. "I sure hope it grows lots of candy canes and mint leaves too!"

"I love chocolate. I really hope this works!" Celesta planted her small chocolate in a bare patch in the garden.

"Ok, I'm going to do it too," said Priscilla. She made a hole with her hand and dropped her small piece of red licorice into the dirt. Then she covered it with the loose soil. "There. I did it."

"You're right, Celesta," said Richard. "I don't want to be selfish. We should try to get more candy so we can share with everyone. Even if it doesn't work, at least we will have tried." Richard planted his purple lollipop. "I guess we'll see what has happened when we wake up in the morning."

Early the next morning, David's voice rang though the castle. "Let's go check our garden!"

Keziah leapt from her bed. "I'm right behind you!"

The children hurried out of their rooms and down the stairs. They opened the heavy door to the courtyard.

"I see some new plants have grown!" cried Priscilla. The children rushed over to the garden.

"But there's no candy on these new plants!" cried David.

"Oh, no!" said Celesta.

"I was right," said Richard. "There's no such thing as a candy tree."

"Now Halloween will have to be cancelled after all," said Priscilla. The children looked sadly at the garden.

"But we could still dress up," said Keziah.

"Good idea!" said Celesta. "We could still have fun. We could have a dress-up party."

"And Daisy could bake a cake," suggested Priscilla.

"A party with no candy," said David sadly.

"Planting our treats was a really nice idea," said Richard. "I think it was good that we tried."

The children went inside and had breakfast.

"Daisy," said Celesta, " could you make a cake for our dress-up party later?"

"Do you children like raspberry cake? I could make you a nice cake with sweet raspberries from the garden."

"That would be great!" said Priscilla.

As they climbed the stairs to their library, for school time with their tutor, the children still felt sad. It just wouldn't be the same, having no Halloween this year.

"We could invite our cousins over for the dress-up party," suggested Keziah.

"That's a great idea!" said Celesta.

"And we could make invitations!" said Priscilla.

"Let's ask our tutor, Mr. Raymond, if we can do it for our art project today," said Richard.

Mr. Raymond thought it was a great idea. "I think I shall dress up as a cat for the party," he said.

David giggled. "That makes sense since…you know." The other children giggled, too.

"Good choice," said Priscilla to Mr. Raymond.

That afternoon, when the invitations were decorated, the children called Nightcat.

"Please take these to our cousins' house," said Celesta.

"We want to invite Mary, Conrad, and Florence to our party," said Priscilla.

"What kind of party are we having?" asked Nightcat.

"A dress-up party!" Keziah said.

"Nightcat, you get to be my horse for the party," said David.

"Do you have a horse costume for me?"

"Of course, My Horse!" said David, grinning and laughing.

Nightcat tried to whinny like a horse. The children giggled.

"I'll go deliver the invitations. I have a feeling that we are going to have a lot of fun this evening." Nightcat took the invitations and left for their cousins' house.

The princes and princesses had an early supper so that they would have time to get ready for the party. After they were finished eating, they all sat around the table a little longer.

"It's too bad you had to cancel Halloween," said Priscilla.

"Yes," said her mother. "But we'll be able to have Halloween next year, once the farmers grow more sugar beets."

"It's too bad no candy trees grew in the garden," said David.

"Maybe we should go and see how those new plants are doing," Keziah suggested.

The children got up from the table and walked out of the kitchen. Richard led the way and opened the door to the courtyard. They could hardly believe the sight that met their eyes. There, right in front of them, was a bubble gum tree with different colored bubble gum fruits on it. Next to it was a candy cane bush covered with multicolored candy canes. Over to the left, there was lollipop bush with lollipops and suckers hanging from it. To the right was a chocolate tree, with large chocolate fruit and, beside it, was a licorice bush with rainbow colored licorice hanging from the ends of its branches.

"Candy!" cried David. "Lots of candy!" The children started picking the candy and dropping it into a nearby wagon.

"It looks like we can have Halloween after all!" cried Priscilla.

"But our parents already cancelled it," said Richard. "It's too late."

"What's too late?" asked Conrad, strolling into the courtyard with Mary and Florence. Their cousins were all dressed up for the party. Mary and Florence were dressed up as cats. Conrad was a dragon.

"What's that?!" asked Florence, pointing at the candy plants in the garden.

"It's candy!" cried David.

"But it's too late to have Halloween. None of the kids from the village will come trick-or-treating because they've already been told it was cancelled," said Mary. Mary was their oldest cousin. She was twelve.

"We can deliver the candy instead!" said Keziah. "The nightcats can pull wagons and we can take candy to every house in the kingdom! It will be like Halloween backwards!"

"Reverse trick-or-treating!" said Celesta.

"That's a great idea!" said Priscilla.

"We'll come with you!" said Florence. "It's going to be so much fun!"

The children finished picking enough candy to fill all three of their wagons. Then the triplets and their brothers went to their rooms to get dressed. They were ready quickly because they had planned their costumes ahead of time. Celesta and Priscilla were dressed up as cats, too. Richard was dressed as a farmer.

"What are you dressed up as?" Conrad asked Keziah.

"Me! I'm dressed up as myself, the way I looked when I rode Nightcat and saved the kingdom from the dragons. Charcoal will be playing the role of Nightcat this evening."

The cousins giggled.

"Nightcat!" yelled David, as he came down the stairs in his costume.

"I'm ready," said Nightcat, landing on the stairs beside him. Nightcat was dressed up as a brown horse. "Neigh, neigh!" said Nightcat.

"Good horse," said David, patting Nightcat on the head.

Charcoal landed beside Keziah. They all walked together to the heavy front doors of the castle.

"I asked our parents and they thought that it was a great idea for us to give out the candy," said Richard. "It will be safe because our nightcats will protect us." Richard pushed the big door open. It was dark outside.

"I'm glad the dragons are gone," said Priscilla. "It's nice to see the stars and not feel scared."

The children walked out into the night, and Mist landed beside Celesta. Richard and Mary attached the wagons full of candies to the big cats. Then they started on their night adventure. They split up. Keziah, Florence and Mary went in one group, with Charcoal. David, Priscilla and Conrad went in Nightcat's group, and Celesta and Richard went with Mist.

The groups went door to door, delivering candy to surprised and excited children. At each house, they yelled trick-or-treat and, when the people inside opened the door to explain that they had no candy, the children gave candy to them! Everyone was so happy. It took a long time to get to all the houses in the whole kingdom. It was almost dawn before the royal children and their cousins saw the castle again. They met outside before going in.

"Let's trick-or-treat at the castle!" said David.

The children laughed and nodded in agreement. They gathered together just outside the big door.

Keziah said, "1, 2, 3…"

"Trick-or-treat!" all the children shouted.

Mr. Raymond opened the door. He was wearing an orange cat costume and had black whiskers painted on his face. With his gold-rimmed glasses, he really did look quite the sight. The children laughed and laughed when they saw what he was wearing.

When the tutor saw the children, his eyes lit up with joy. "Children! There you are! I've been waiting for the dress-up party!"

"And, guess what, Mr. Raymond, we have candy! There's lots left over!" said David. "It's time to party!"

They all went into the great ballroom which Daisy and Mr. Raymond had decorated. There they played games, danced around, and ate raspberry cake and candy. Daisy and their parents got out of bed and joined them. They were wearing cat costumes too.

"This was the best Halloween we've ever had at Kitty Castle!" said Keziah, and everyone agreed!

CHRISTMAS

It was Christmas Eve and the princes and princesses of Kitty Castle were sitting together in the library.

"What do you want for Christmas?" asked Princess Priscilla. Priscilla and her two sisters were triplets. They were eight years old. Their older brother, Richard, was twelve. Their younger brother, David, was six.

"I want toys," said David. "I really think we have enough cats now so, no offense Nightcat, but I really hope we don't get any more. It's annoying to hear them meowing all the time."

"I hope you get toys too," said Nightcat. Nightcat was their pet. He used to be just a normal silver cat but, after drinking the magic water under Kitty Castle, he got much bigger and grew wings.

"What toy do you want?" asked Princess Keziah.

"I want a toy train," said David.

"I'd like a beautiful doll," said Priscilla.

"I'd like a toy horse with hair," said Celesta.

"I'd like a toy dragon," said Keziah.

"A dragon?!" exclaimed Richard. "Why would you ever want that? Dragons have caused nothing but trouble in the kingdom!"

"Well, I still think they're cool. Maybe we'll find a good dragon one day."

Nightcat felt worried. He didn't have anything to give to the children for Christmas. How could he make them happy if he couldn't give them what they wanted?

Mr. Raymond walked over to their table, looked at the group and adjusted his golden-rimmed spectacles. "That's all for today, Students. Good work everyone." His eyes met each of the children's eyes in turn but, when he came to Nightcat, he just looked away. Their tutor had no imagination so he couldn't understand anything magical, not even Nightcat. Once he had thought Nightcat was a bear but, now, it was like he couldn't see him at all.

"Yes!" said David. "Let's go outside and play in the snow!"

The other children agreed and they raced down the stairs to the main hall to put on their winter gear. Once they were ready, Richard pushed open the heavy front door of the castle. Outside, everything was covered in a thick layer of sparkling white snow. It was just the right temperature. The snow was perfect for making snowmen!

"I love winter," said Nightcat. "The snow is so soft. I feel like I could just sleep out here." He snuggled into the wet, sticky snow.

"It's cold," Keziah said.

"Not for me," said Nightcat.

"That's because you have thick fur," said Richard.

"And because you're magical," said Celesta.

"Let's make a snowcat," said Priscilla.

"Great idea!" said Nightcat. All the children agreed. They got to work building a snowcat.

Suddenly, they heard the sound of jingling bells. Nightcat looked up and saw a red sleigh in the sky. The children stopped playing in the snow and looked up too. The sleigh was flying towards the castle! Reindeer, with bells on their harnesses, pulled the sleigh. "I wonder who is in the sleigh," said Richard. The jingling sound got louder as the sleigh got closer. Soon it landed in the snow in front of the castle. The reindeer pranced to a stop.

The king and queen hurried out the castle door to meet the visitors. "Welcome," boomed the king.

Little men with long beards jumped down from the sleigh. They were dressed in green. "We are elves from the north," said one of the little men.

"Welcome," said the queen. "Why have you come?"

"We heard about your giant magical cat and we wanted to meet him."

"Hi," said Nightcat. He walked over to the little elves.

The elves bowed to Nightcat. "We have heard of your courage and your goodness. Please come back with us and be our leader. You can be our king!"

The children gasped.

"Oh no!" cried Priscilla.

"No way!" said David.

"Hush, Children," said the queen. "This is for Nightcat to decide."

"But he *can't* leave," said David. "He's *our* pet!"

"This is a serious matter," said the king. "Let's talk about it inside."

"Maybe you would like to stay with us for a while," the queen said to the elves.

"We thank you for your kind offer. Nightcat, we will wait for your answer for the rest of the day. Should you decide to become our king, all of these toys will be yours." The elf pointed to the big red bag in the back of the sleigh. "We will stay with you until tonight."

"Only one day!" cried Nightcat. "That's not long enough to make such an important decision."

"I can't believe you'd even consider it!" said Celesta.

"But, if I became their king, maybe I could really help them. And look at all the toys I'd be able to give you for Christmas!"

"You have until this evening to decide, Nightcat," said one of the elves. "Can we keep our reindeer in your barn so they don't fly away?" he asked the king.

"Yes, of course," answered the king.

The elves unhitched their reindeer. Nightcat offered to take the reindeer to the barn so the elves went into the castle with the king and the queen. The children were too upset to finish their snow sculpture so they went inside too.

"I hope their reindeer fly away," said David.

"David, that's not very nice," scolded Celesta.

"Well, I hope so too," said Keziah. The children went sadly to their rooms.

Nightcat led the reindeer to the barn.

"Nice place you've got here." One of the reindeer had spoken!

"You can talk?!" asked Nightcat.

"Of course. All magical, flying creatures can talk."

"I didn't know that. What's it like, where you're from?" asked Nightcat.

"It snows all the time. And it's very loud because the elves are always making toys. And they fight a lot too. I'm Prancer, by the way."

"What do you think? Do you think I should come back with you?"

"We think you should come with us. These elves need help! Isn't that right, Comet?" said Prancer.

"Yes, they really do. And just take a look in the bag on the sleigh! Just look at all the toys you could give the kids. It's really too bad that the elves make so many toys and usually just keep them all for themselves."

Nightcat walked over to the sleigh and looked into the bag. There he saw a beautiful toy horse with hair, a deluxe train set, a lovely doll, a toy dragon and many other wonderful kinds of toys he had never seen before. "These would be perfect gifts for the children!"

"We sure hope you'll be able to come and be our king," said Prancer. "You'll be so famous! Maybe you could even lead our sleigh sometimes."

"Yes!" said Comet. "If you become our king, we'll all bow to you everyday."

"I'll have to think about that," said Nightcat. He thought it would be cool to lead the sleigh and to have people bowing to him. Maybe he was getting tired of just being a pet.

Nightcat said goodbye to the reindeer and returned to the castle. Inside, he headed towards the children's rooms. He stopped outside the door of their common area because he heard them talking.

"I can't believe Nightcat is even thinking about it!" said Keziah.

"Well, he's a very important cat," said Richard. "Maybe he has other important things he needs to do."

"He's *our* important cat!" cried David.

"I wish Great Aunt Esmeralda and Mist and Charcoal were here. They would help him to make the right decision," said Priscilla.

"The right decision is obvious. He should stay with us," said Celesta.

"We don't know *anything* about these elves. They're strangers," said Keziah.

"But still, maybe it's a good opportunity," said Richard.

"Richard, don't tell me you want him to go," said Keziah.

"I'm just saying that we have to let him choose."

"But we need him!" said Priscilla.

"Well, who cares about him anyway?" said David. "Maybe we have too many pet cats!" An inside door slammed.

Nightcat hurried away, down the stairs. He just couldn't face the children like this. They were mad at him. He felt sad and confused. Had he done something wrong? What was the right choice?

He walked out into the courtyard. There were walls all the way around and a magical garden in the center. No snow covered the magical garden. The garden was growing, even in the winter. Nightcat looked at the candy trees that grew in the garden and smiled. There was a whole tree of candy canes. He could tape some onto the children's presents. That's when Nightcat realized that he was planning to go with the elves. Then he could give those nice toys to the children. And maybe they didn't really want him to stay anyway. Plus, being king sounded more important than being a pet.

That evening, the elves put on a Christmas concert. Everyone in Kitty Kingdom was invited. Most people were excited for the concert. The king and queen gave out candy canes from their magic tree to all of the children. But the princes and princesses were very unhappy.

"When are you going to decide?" Celesta asked Nightcat.

"Let's just enjoy this music together," said Nightcat. "We can talk about it more later." He didn't want to tell her that he had already decided to go with the elves.

Everyone gathered in the grand ballroom to watch the concert. The princes and princesses sat together in the front row. The elves asked Nightcat to come up onto the stage. He was surprised that he was going to be part of the show. The elves led Nightcat to a throne and asked him to sit on it. Nightcat smiled as he looked out at all the people. It was fun being the king! Then the elves started singing. Nightcat recognized the songs but some of the words were different. First they sang "Jingle Bells".

Dashing through the snow

In a one-cat open sleigh

O'er the fields we go

Laughing all the way

Bells on bobtail ring

Making spirits bright

What fun it is to ride and sing

A sleighing song tonight!

Jingle bells, jingle bells,

Jingle all the way.

Oh! what fun it is to ride

In a one-cat open sleigh.

Jingle bells, jingle bells,

Jingle all the way;

Oh! what fun it is to ride

In a one-cat open sleigh.

Nightcat smiled and sang along. It was fun being the center of all the attention. Then they sang "O Nightcat", to the tune of "O Christmas Tree".

O Nightcat! O Nightcat!
Your powers are amazing;
O Nightcat! O Nightcat!
Your powers are amazing;

Not only when the summer's here,
But also when 'tis cold and drear.
O Nightcat! O Nightcat!
Your powers are amazing!

After the song, Nightcat felt a little bad. Christmas wasn't supposed to be all about him, was it? Then they sang another song about Nightcat. This was turning out to be a very odd kind of Christmas sing-along.

Jolly old King Nightcat,
lean your ear this way!
Don't you tell a single soul,
what I'm going to say;
Christmas Day is coming soon;
if you don't come now;
What will you give the kids
sitting in the crowd?

Hurry up and make your choice,

it's almost time to go,

We'll make our reindeer bow to you,

you want that, don't you know?

We will make you our king and

we'll give you gold,

Then you'll make us famous,

as has been foretold.

While they were singing, Nightcat started to worry about what life would be like there. They wouldn't love him like the children did. Making the elves famous wouldn't really be helping them. He had thought he would be going to help them. Would these elves even listen to him at all? He was getting a bad feeling about it.

Next, the elves sang their version of "Up on the Rooftop".

Up on the rooftop reindeer pause
Often some mischief we like to cause
With you we'll make a lot of toys
All for our own Christmas joys

Oh, oh, oh!
Who wouldn't go!
Oh, oh, oh!
Who wouldn't go!
With us, the naughty elves
Click, click, click
We're flying north soon
Make your pick!

The naughty elves! As Nightcat listened to the words of their song, he realized that he wouldn't be able to help these elves. He didn't want to be the king of the naughty elves! Then he looked out at the princes and princesses sitting in the front row. They looked so sad.

The elves finished their performance with their version of "We wish you a Merry Christmas".

We wish you a Merry Christmas
We wish you a Merry Christmas
We wish you a Merry Christmas
And a Happy New Year

Good tidings we'll bring
If you'll be our king,
Good tidings for Christmas
And a Happy New Year

Nightcat couldn't concentrate on the words. He was thinking that going with the elves wasn't the best idea after all. But what could he give the children if he didn't agree to go with the elves?

Then Nightcat remembered the true story of Christmas. It happened in a different time and a different place. But he knew it was true. The One True King had given himself as a gift to the people, to save the whole world. Suddenly Nightcat knew what he could do! He could give himself as a gift to the children! Even though he couldn't save the whole world as the One True King had done, he *could* give his love and himself to his friends. The naughty elves would have to get someone else to be their king.

After the concert, he went outside with the elves.

"I'm not coming with you," Nightcat said.

"We are very angry!" yelled one of the elves.

"No gold or toys for you," said another one. Then they all threw snow at Nightcat.

He sneezed and laughed at the angry little fellows. "I'm sorry you're mad, but I have important work to do here in Kitty Kingdom."

The elves got their reindeer ready and flew away in a huff. The bells on their sleigh jingled as they went.

Then Nightcat went back inside the castle. The concert had ended late so all the children were in bed. "This is my chance," he whispered. He dragged a very large box out of the storage room, up the stairs and into the library. Then he wrapped the box with red sparkly wrapping paper. He wrapped the lid of the box separately and taped candy canes on top. On the lid, he wrote **From**

Nightcat. Then he jumped inside and pulled the lid down over the top of the box. He curled up and went to sleep. Soon it would be Christmas morning.

The princes and princesses came into the library early the next morning.

"Do you think Nightcat left?" asked Keziah.

"I haven't seen him since the concert," said Priscilla.

"Wow! Look at that huge present!" cried David. The children all crowded around the giant gift.

"He must have left," said Celesta, starting to cry.

"And he didn't even say goodbye," said Richard.

"I can't believe it!" said David, crossing his arms. "Who cares about toys if we don't have Nightcat!" He kicked the big present.

"Well, let's see what he left us," said Keziah, sadly. She pulled the lid off.

"Surprise!" Nightcat sprang out.

The children laughed. "Nightcat!" they cried.

"I'm so happy to see you!" said Celesta.

"I gave myself as a gift to you," said Nightcat. "I love you! I'm always going to stay with you and be your pet."

The children all hugged Nightcat and he purred loudly.

"Let's sing the elves' naughty song," said David. "It's funny!"

"I don't want to," said Nightcat. "I hope I never have to hear those songs again! Let's sing a real Christmas song instead." So Nightcat and the children sang Joy to the World, a song about the One True King.

Joy to the world, the Lord is come!
Let earth receive her King;
Let every heart prepare Him room,
And Heaven and nature sing,
And Heaven and nature sing,
And Heaven, and Heaven,

               and nature sing.

Joy to the earth, the Savior reigns!

Let men their songs employ;

While fields and floods, rocks,

                      hills and plains

Repeat the sounding joy,

Repeat the sounding joy,

Repeat, repeat, the sounding joy.

He rules the world with truth and grace,

And makes the nations prove

The glories of His righteousness,

And wonders of His love,

And wonders of His love,

And wonders, wonders, of His love.

Love is the best gift of all. As they sang, they all felt the true joy of Christmas. Nightcat knew that he had made the right choice.

NIGHTCAT LEARNS TO READ

It was almost time for the I Love to Read month at Kitty Castle. The princess and princes were very excited about it. In fact, the whole kingdom was excited. I Love to Read was one of the biggest celebrations of the year!

Richard, David, Priscilla, Celesta and Keziah were in the library, sitting around a table together. They were choosing books to read to younger children who would attend the celebration.

"But I can't celebrate. I don't know how to read," said Nightcat. Nightcat was a grey cat with furry wings. He had green eyes and was about the size of a tiger.

"That's okay," said Celesta. "David can't read very well yet either, because he just turned six." All three princesses were eight-years-old. They were triplets. Princess Celesta had blonde curly hair and brown eyes.

"But I'm older than six. And I can't read at all!" said Nightcat. He looked at the children sadly. "What if I can never learn because I'm a cat?"

"If you say things like that, then you'll never be able to do it!" said Keziah. "I've learned that!" Princess Keziah had brown curly hair and brown eyes.

"You need to just keep trying," said David. "That's what I do." Prince David had blond hair and brown eyes.

"Nightcat doesn't know the letters," Richard said. Prince Richard was the oldest. He was eleven and had short brown hair and brown eyes. "We should teach him!"

"How should we start?" asked David. "With the A,B,C song?"

"That won't help him with knowing how the letters sound," said Keziah.

"That would only help him know what the letters are called."

"We need letter flashcards," said Celesta.

"Our tutor has them," said David. "He used them with me to help me learn the letter sounds."

"Let's get them!" said Priscilla.

"Only…what will we tell Mr. Raymond?" asked Celesta. Mr. Raymond was their tutor. He was a tall man with golden-rimmed spectacles. He had no imagination. So he couldn't see anything magical, not even Nightcat.

"I'll tell him that we want to test someone to make sure he knows all the letter sounds. Mr. Raymond will probably think we are testing David or some other kid in the kingdom, to help them learn to read," said Keziah.

"Good idea!" said David.

The children went to find their tutor. Mr. Raymond gave them the letter flashcards and the children went straight back to Nightcat.

"We got them!" exclaimed David.

The children sat down at the table while Nightcat looked at the flashcards curiously. "Those little papers will give me the ability to read?"

"These are letters," said Keziah.

"Letters will give me the ability to read?"

"It's not magical," said Richard. "Nothing can just give you the ability to read. You have to learn how to do it and then practice a lot."

"You need to know what sounds the letters make so you can put them together to make a word," explained Keziah.

Celesta took the letter 'b' and showed it to Nightcat. She told him the name of the letter and that 'b' says, 'buh'.

Nightcat looked at her in confusion. "It says, 'buh'? That's funny. I didn't hear that paper say anything. *You* said 'buh'!"

"Nightcat, if you read the letter in a book, it says, 'buh'," Keziah explained.

"I've never heard a book say anything either," grumbled Nightcat. "This learning to read is hard!"

"No, Nightcat! The book doesn't talk! You read the letter 'b' and *you* say, 'buh'. Once you get enough letters in your head, you'll be able to form a word. So when you see a "b", you think 'buh' and then you look at the next letter," said Keziah.

"Is there an easier way to start?" asked Nightcat.

"Maybe we should teach him to read his own name first," suggested Priscilla.

"Good idea," said David. "I think my name is the first word that I learned to read."

Richard took a small chalkboard and wrote, 'Nightcat'. "Here. This is your name." He held the chalkboard up so Nightcat could see it."

"That's my name? I like it!"

The children worked with Nightcat to teach him to read. Everyday, he learned a little bit more. Soon it was time for the I Love to Read Celebration. Many people were invited to Kitty Castle for a huge party to start the I Love to Read month. The children watched as the guests walked into the ballroom.

"But I still can't read," said Nightcat. "All I know is my name and a few letters!"

"That's okay," said David. "When you're learning to read, it doesn't happen all at once. It takes years for you to get better and better. But it can be fun. It's like a learn-to-read adventure!"

Just then, they heard a loud commotion coming from out in the hall.

"Oh, no," said Celesta. "I hope it's not dragons!"

The children rushed out to see what was making the noise. There, just inside the castle, was an enormous worm, thrashing around and whacking itself against the door and the wall.

"Everybody get back!" shouted the king.

"What's going on?!" asked Nightcat.

The worm stopped and gasped, "I wasn't invited to the party! Because I can't read!" Then he started thrashing again and wailing loudly. "And I'm a book worm," he sobbed.

"Wait!" said Priscilla. "You could learn!"

"Yeah," shouted David so the worm would hear him, "I only just learned to read! You could learn too!"

"And I'm only learning now," said Nightcat. "We could learn together."

The worm stopped crying and looked at Nightcat and the children. "You could teach me how to read?"

"Yes!" said the children all together.

"And could I come to the party, too?"

"Of course you are welcome at the party," said the King.

They all went into the party and the bookworm behaved himself very nicely.

"I love this learn-to-read adventure!" said Keziah, laughing. "We have so much fun together!"

VALENTINES

Chapter 1

It all started with a kiss – a chocolate kiss. It was almost time for the Friendship Festival at Kitty Castle. The two princes and three princesses were in the kitchen making chocolate treats for all their friends and relatives.

"I wonder if night cats are the only magical creatures in Kitty Kingdom," said

Princess Celesta. She had long, blond, curly hair and brown eyes.

"I don't know," said Princess Priscilla. The three sisters were triplets. They were eight years old.

"What other magical creatures could there be?" asked Prince David. He had blond hair and blue eyes. David was five years old, the youngest of the family.

"What about that dragon in the dungeon?" asked Prince Richard. "Isn't it odd that he's not turning back into a kitten?"

Cats that stay up all night, every night, are night cats. Night cats are magical and they turn into magical creatures. If a night cat is treated well, it will turn into a huge, tiger-sized cat with wings! (That's what happened to their own pet, Nightcat.) But if a night cat is treated badly, it will turn into a dragon. Night cat dragons can be changed back into kittens by splashing them with magic water from a pool that lies deep under Kitty Castle.

"I wonder why the magic water isn't working on that dragon," said Princess Keziah.

"I feel sorry for him. We splashed him with magic water so many times and it's just not working. I wish we didn't have to keep him in the dungeon," said Celesta.

"What other choice do we have?" asked Keziah.

"Maybe we could make the dragon some treats too," suggested Priscilla.

"What kind of treats?" asked David.

"How about a giant chocolate kiss?" suggested Celesta.

"Great idea!" said Priscilla.

"Wait a minute. I know chocolate isn't good for dogs. Is it okay for dragons?" asked Richard.

"I know it's okay for Nightcat – he told me that it was. So it must be okay for dragons because they're magical too," said Keziah.

"Maybe if we're kind to the dragon, he'll finally turn back into a kitten," said Priscilla.

"It's worth a try," said Richard.

So the children started making a giant chocolate kiss for the dragon in the dungeon.

***

"It's cold down here," said Priscilla.

"And it's damp too," complained David.

"I thought it would be hot, considering we've got a dragon trapped down here," said Keziah.

The children were going slowly down the stairs to the dungeon, all helping to carry the giant chocolate kiss.

"Where's Nightcat?" asked Celesta.

"I think he's decorating for the Friendship Festival," said Keziah.

They reached the bottom of the stairs and started down the long passageway to the cell. When they arrived at the door, they realized that the kiss was way too big to fit through the food slot.

"How are we going to get this in to him?" asked David.

The huge red dragon was curled up, with his eyes closed, on the far side of the cell. His scales were like polished Jasper stones. He had double horns on each side of his head. One of his horns had a crack through it. His claws were long and black.

"He's sleeping," said Priscilla. "Aww…He looks kinda cute when he's sleeping. Poor little thing."

"Maybe we could open the door just a crack and shove the kiss inside," suggested Celesta.

"I don't think that's a good idea. What if the dragon wakes up? What if he hears the door opening?" Richard protested.

"We'll be quick," said David.

The children were silent as they thought about the idea for a moment.

"I think we should try it," said Priscilla. "Quickly, before the dragon wakes up."

"Okay." Richard took the heavy key ring off the hook on the wall. Quietly, he found the right key and slipped it into the keyhole. He turned the key slowly so that it didn't make a loud sound. When the door unlocked, there was a soft click.

None of the children had noticed that one of the dragon's eyes was now half open. Jasper Flame had been watching their every move, hoping that they would all agree to open the door. As soon as they opened it a little, to push the chocolate in, the dragon sprang up and leapt towards the partially open door. Richard tried to push the door closed but he was too slow and not strong enough to hold back the powerful dragon. The door flew open. The dragon burst out into the corridor.

"Nightcat!" the children screamed.

The dragon pushed past, knocking them over, and then scrambled towards the stairs. He bounded up them and, as soon as he got to the top, he opened his wings and blew a stream of super-heated fire towards the large wooden doors of the castle. The doors burst into flames and then collapsed as the dragon flew through the burning debris and out into the evening sky. The sun was just setting.

Jasper Flame's powerful wings beat the air. Freedom! They had tortured him with water and, just now, they had tried to poison him. They would pay! He would see to that! His scales were still hurting from that water torture. If dragons get water on their scales, it hurts.

And they had poured water on him again and again and again. And they had chanted, "Turn into a kitten." Why would he want to turn into a kitten? They were insane and dangerous! He had to protect his tribe. Most of the other dragons were much younger. Thank goodness those other, strange dragons had left but it was still hard to find food, especially with those big, flying cats around. The strange dragons had burned most of the forest and fields. The prey that he hunted depended on those habitats, so, now, food was scarce. That's how he'd gotten caught in the first place. He had been hunting too close to people. The giant cat had breathed sparkles on him, which had made it hard for him to breathe. Then they had splashed him with water for the first time. After he had been taken, the splashing continued.

Jasper looked behind him as he flew. He didn't see anyone following him. But it was almost dark now. Would he be able to see those giant cats if they were there? Maybe he shouldn't go home just yet. What if they were following him? But he decided to take the risk. He needed to check on the rest of his tribe.

He changed course and flew towards home. It was dark night now and only the stars twinkled above him. There was no moon in the sky. He flew quickly. Soon he saw the large, dark shadow of an extinct volcano below him. Jasper flew down into the middle of the opening. He landed with a quiet thud and sent up a call to summon the dragons. Soon all the dragons there had gathered around Jasper.

"Family, I'm sorry that I have been gone so long. I was captured. The giant cats with wings captured me and children tortured me in their dungeon."

The dragons around him gasped. One young dragonlet started to snivel.

"We're dragons. We don't cry. We fight!"

At this, the other dragons erupted in chaos. Jasper waited for them to quiet down.

"What do we do now?" asked a dragon.

"We make a plan."

Chapter 2

Jasper always did his best thinking while flying. After dismissing the crowd, he leapt up into the air. He flew all night long. Finally, he knew what he had to do. He landed in an isolated meadow to consider his plan.

"I need to capture one of the flying cats," he said.

"I can help with that!" A leprechaun popped into view. He was wee little man, the size of a young child, dressed all in minty green. And his skin was green too! His blue eyes sparkled. "Wouldn't you like some help?"

"How could you help me capture a flying cat? And why would you even want to, for that matter?"

"Well, you see, they didn't invite me to the Friendship Festival because it isn't my holiday. But they invited some other people even though Valentine's Day isn't their holiday either. Like the bookworm and…lots of others too." He finished in a huff and crossed his arms. "They should have invited me to their party. Now it's time to teach them a lesson!"

"And, now, to the other question. How can you help me?"

"The name's Gold, by the way."

"Why are you called Gold? You're all green!"

He stomped his foot. "I had a pot of gold but those meddling castle dwellers stole it from me!"

"My name is Jasper Flame."

Another dragon landed lightly in the meadow. "My name is Electric Ruby!" Her scales looked like gleaming rubies and her blue eyes were full of electric fire. Her horns were single and more to the top of her head, as compared to Jasper's.

Her long, slender tail had six spikes on the end of it – three on each side. "I overheard your conversation as I was circling high above this meadow. My tribe was scattered during the great fires set by the castle dragons. Now I am alone."

"Hello, Ruby," said Jasper. Dragons always went by their gem name except when they first introduced themselves or in a formal setting.

"The castle dragons?" asked Gold.

"Those other, weird dragons must have come from the castle. They ruined my life."

"They will pay for what they've done," said Jasper.

"It's nice to meet you." Gold made a fancy bow. "But now, to the plan. First of all, how will we avoid Nightcat's magic sleeping dust?" asked Gold.

"Oh, that dust can't work on dragons, since we have magic in our scales," said Ruby.

"But what if it gets inside your mouth? You don't have scales in your throat!"

The dragons looked at Gold for a moment and then burst out laughing.

"How would we blow fire if we didn't have scales in our throat and mouths? We'd set ourselves on fire from the inside!" said Jasper.

"Well, isn't that lucky for you," said the leprechaun. "I found out the hard way - that horrible glitter dust works on me!"

"Did they trap you?" asked Ruby.

"They put me in prison. But as soon as I woke up, I got away."

"How did you do that?" asked Ruby.

"I shrank and walked out through the bars."

"Shrank?" echoed Ruby.

"Of course. Leprechauns can shrink, don't you know."

"Then show me!" said Jasper.

"I think not. Let's get back to business."

"Then I won't believe you can shrink. You probably never even got captured by them. You look like one of them anyway."

"One of what?" asked Gold.

"One of the humans."

"Yeah, you do," said Ruby.

"I do not! Just look at me! I'm a leprechaun!" He stomped his foot again.

"You look like a small human, dyed green. And that's probably what they thought you were!" said Ruby.

"Hmm…that might explain why they were so silly as to let me get away. But I'll get my gold back."

"What gold?" asked Jasper.

"All the gold in the kingdom belongs me. I'll get back my pot of gold and all the rest too. Gold belongs to leprechauns, don't you know. And I'm the only one."

The dragons looked at each other. Jasper opened his mouth to say something but Ruby shook her head at him. They both had piles of treasure at home but they didn't want the leprechaun to steal all of *their* gold.

"So they put you in the dungeon for stealing gold?" asked Jasper.

"Not stealing! Reclaiming! ALL the gold belongs to me," Gold insisted.

"All gems used to belong to the dragons. But you don't see us stealing," said Jasper.

Ruby interrupted their fight. "Anyway, time for a plan. How can we get revenge for what they did to us?"

"We should capture Nightcat. He's a danger to all magical creatures, everywhere," said Gold.

"Good idea," said Ruby. "How and when?"

"That celebration that they're having – the big cat will certainly be out helping to deliver invitations," said Jasper.

"Perfect opportunity to trap him when he's off by himself," said Gold.

They all laughed.

Chapter 3

Nightcat was flying high in the sky. It was a beautiful, sunny day! He had a bag full of invitations, for the Valentine's Day Friendship Festival, to deliver to the townspeople.

"This will be such a happy celebration! And all the people in Kitty Kingdom will be invited!"

Little did Nightcat realize that dragons were stealthily flying up behind him.

"Inviting everyone but us, aren't you?" screeched Ruby.

"What?" Nightcat turned to see who was behind him, which was a mistake. The dragons blew fire at him. Nightcat tried to fly faster. The invitations started spilling out of the large bag he was carrying. Gold, who was on the ground, collected the invitations so that no one would find them.

Nightcat blew sparkles from his mouth. That was one of his superpowers. The sparkle dust usually put everyone asleep. But the dragons didn't even slow down.

"Oh, you're *that* dragon. My sparkles don't work on you. We were wondering where you went! Why are you chasing me?" But the dragons didn't answer. The sparkle dust that Nightcat had breathed floated down and landed on Gold, putting him fast asleep.

Nightcat was flying as fast as he could. But he couldn't get away from the dragons. Soon all the invitations had spilled out and his bag was empty. Ruby grabbed the bag away from him. Jasper flew right into Nightcat, pushing him. Ruby opened the huge bag and caught him in his own bag. Quickly she zipped it up so Nightcat couldn't get out.

"Why are you doing this?" came Nightcat's muffled voice from inside the bag.

"We're protecting all the magic creatures of Kitty Kingdom," said Jasper.

Nightcat clawed at the bag, trying to get out. "I didn't do anything!"

"What about putting me in prison and splashing me with water?"

"We were just trying to turn you back!" Nightcat protested.

"Back to what?"

"Back into a kitten!"

The dragons laughed. "That's the silliest thing I ever heard," said Ruby.

Ruby and Jasper carried the bag into a nearby cave. Then Ruby went back for the leprechaun, who was just waking up on the grassy meadow.

As Ruby and the leprechaun entered the cave, Gold said, "You caught him! Now what? I think we should hold him ransom and demand all the gold in Kitty Kingdom."

"That wasn't part of the plan," said Ruby.

"Some of us don't want all the gold in Kitty Kingdom," said Jasper.

Gold stomped angrily. "Then, what *is* the plan?"

"Maybe we can ruin their celebration," said Jasper.

"Why would you want to do that?" asked Nightcat from inside the bag.

"We told you. We're punishing all of you for putting me into prison for no reason!"

"Hey, I think I'm suffocating in here."

"Like we care!" said Gold.

"So what?" said Jasper.

"You guys are mean! I didn't know we had bad guys in Kitty Kingdom!"

"We're not the bad guys! *You're* the bad guy! You're the one that put me in prison for no reason! And you tortured me by splashing me with water! My scales are still hurting! Then those kids tried to poison me with chocolate! You're the bad guys!" said Jasper.

Nightcat sighed. "Let me out so we can talk about this."

"No way! You'd try to attack us and fly away," said Ruby.

"I promise I won't hurt you," said Nightcat.

Ruby laughed. "We don't trust you."

"We could tie him up with the bag so he can't get away," said Jasper.

"We could also move some stones to block the entrance," said Ruby.

"Good idea," said Jasper. So the two dragons moved some large stones to block most of the entrance to the cave so that Nightcat couldn't get out.

"But now you've trapped us in here too," Gold whined.

"We can move them once we put him back in the bag," said Jasper.

They let Nightcat out and then quickly tied him up with the large bag.

"Phew! That's better! Now we can talk," said Nightcat.

"Forget it. We're going home to sleep," said Jasper.

"We're leaving you here all night. Maybe then, we'll talk," said Ruby.

The dragons moved the boulders. Gold, Ruby and Jasper walked out of the cave. Then the dragons put the large stones back into place, covering the entrance to the cave. Luckily, Nightcat wasn't afraid. He could see perfectly in the dark and he knew his friends would come to help him.

In the morning, the dragons and Gold returned. They had just entered the cave and pushed the boulders back into place when the boulders started moving again.

"What?!" cried Gold.

"Someone's pushing the stones! But who?" asked Jasper.

The boulders lurched away from the cave entrance. There stood a copy of Nightcat.

"Dad!" cried Nightcat.

"We're here to rescue you!" Charcoal tried blowing sparkle dust at the dragons.

"Dad! That doesn't work on them. It just makes them mad!"

"We're already mad," roared Ruby as she tried to breathe fire at the intruder. Charcoal dodged out of the way.

Charcoal and Mist rushed into the cave, ready to fight for their son. The dragons surrounded Nightcat to make sure he couldn't escape.

"Wait!" cried Nightcat. "Let's talk about this."

"No!" Jasper roared.

"Let's talk," said Ruby. "If we fight like this, we might end up getting hurt badly."

Jasper frowned at her. He didn't want to look weak in front of the others. But he knew she was right.

Just then, Great Aunt Esmeralda strode into the cave, followed by the princes and princesses.

At the sight of the princesses, Jasper said, "Well, if it isn't the ones who tried to poison me. Lucky I got away or I could be dead right now."

Princess Celesta started crying. "We weren't trying to hurt you! We were trying to be nice!"

Princess Pricilla, on hearing her sister, started crying too. "Why are you trying to hurt Nightcat? We love him!"

"You hurt me by splashing water on me and keeping me trapped in your dungeon," Jasper retorted.

Ruby felt sorry for the crying little girls and, for the first time, she started to wonder if, maybe, they *were* being the bad guys.

"We were just trying to turn you back into a cute kitten. You'd be much cuter as a kitten. We were trying to save you! And why didn't it work, by the way? The magic water works on everything! Even people!"

"We're magic, really magic. Magic doesn't work on magic."

Great Aunt Esmeralda spoke. "We did not realize you were true dragons. Please forgive us. We're very sorry."

"But my whole tribe was driven away by those other strange dragons you brought here," said Ruby.

"We didn't bring those dragons here!" said Keziah. "We got rid of all those crazy dragons by turning them into kittens!"

"Maybe we can help you find your tribe!" said Richard.

"We certainly can," said Great Aunt Esmeralda.

Just at that moment, they all heard a sound coming from one side of the cave. Snoring. It was Gold, fast asleep!

Everyone laughed at the sight of the tiny leprechaun, all curled up on the floor, snoring like an earthquake.

"I see the sparkle dust worked on someone! I thought that sound was a tractor!" said David. They all laughed again.

With an extra loud snort, Gold woke up, rubbing his eyes. "What? Huh? I wasn't sleeping."

Jasper and Ruby looked into each other's eyes.

"Fine, We accept your apology. But we want you to help Ruby find her tribe and then leave us and all our dragon-kind alone," said Jasper

"Agreed," said Great Aunt Esmeralda.

"And you'll all be invited to the Friendship Festival!" Priscilla said.

"What about my gold?!" the leprechaun shouted.

"What gold?" asked Richard.

"All the gold in the kingdom belongs to me!"

"Now, that's just silly," said Ruby.

"That's right, Gold. Not all the gold belongs to you. Dragons have gold too and have had from ages past," said Jasper

Gold burst into tears. "I don't have any gold at all. Someone stole the gold I kept at the end of the rainbow."

The princes and princesses looked at each other.

"It was us," confessed Richard.

"But we didn't know it was yours!" said David.

"We're sorry," said Priscilla.

"We'll give it back," said Celesta.

"Really? You would do that?" asked Gold.

"Yes, of course," said Keziah.

Gold wiped his tears away. "Okay."

"It's settled then," said Great Aunt Esmeralda. "We need to get the invitations delivered before it's too late for everyone to get to the Friendship Festival. The party is this evening."

Ruby untied Nightcat. "Maybe we can help!" said Ruby.

"Sure!" said Nightcat. "Gold, do you want to ride on my back to help deliver the invitations?"

Gold jumped up and down and did a summersault in the air. "I've never been flying before!"

"Okay, let's go!" said Nightcat. They all went outside and raced around, gathering up the invitations from where they had fallen when Nightcat was captured.

"This is how we found you," said Celesta, as she gathered the last of the colorful envelopes. "We saw the invitations on the grass here."

"Then we followed some dragon footprints," said David.

"I was gathering up the invitations, only I fell asleep, because *someone* blew sparkles everywhere," said Gold

Nightcat laughed. "Sorry about that, Little Buddy." Nightcat licked the leprechaun. Gold fell over. "Oops. Sorry about that." Everyone laughed and, this time, Gold laughed too. Then the children and Gold got onto the night cats' backs.

"Can I invite my family to the Friendship Festival?" asked Jasper.

"Of course!" said Nightcat.

They took to the air, to deliver the invitations. The children, the night cats, the dragons and the leprechaun all knew that this was already the perfect Valentine's Day because they had made new friends.

KITTY CASTLE BOOKS

Get all the Kitty Castle books on Amazon.com!

KITTY CASTLE 1 - NIGHTCAT

KITTY CASTLE 2 - SURPRISES!

KITTY CASTLE 3 - ANSWERS!

KITTY CASTLE 4 - MYSTERY!

KITTY CASTLE 5 – REUNION

KITTY CASTLE 6 - CELEBRATIONS

If you liked this book, please leave us a great review on Amazon.com! Thanks for reading!

Bruce County Public Library
1243 Mackenzie Rd.
Port Elgin ON N0H 2C6

CPSIA information can be obtained at www.ICGtesting.com
Printed in the USA
LVOW07s0048050915

452957LV00001B/25/P

9 781503 082342